Bedtime Stories for Kids

Calming Short Stories for Kids, Children, and Toddlers to Help Them Fall Asleep Fast, Reduce Anxiety, and Learn Mindfulness Meditation

Unicorns, Fairy Tales, and More!

PUBLISHED BY: Kaizen Mindfulness Meditations

© **Copyright 2019 - All rights reserved.**

The content contained within this book may not be reproduced, duplicated or transmitted without direct written permission from the author or the publisher.

Under no circumstances will any blame or legal responsibility be held against the publisher, or author, for any damages, reparation, or monetary loss due to the information contained within this book. Either directly or indirectly.

Legal Notice:

This book is copyright protected. This book is only for personal use. You cannot amend, distribute, sell, use, quote or paraphrase any part, or the content within this book, without the consent of the author or publisher.

Disclaimer Notice:

Please note the information contained within this document is for educational and entertainment purposes only. All effort has been executed to present accurate, up to date, and reliable, complete information. No warranties of any kind are declared or implied. Readers acknowledge that the author is not engaging in the rendering of legal, financial, medical or professional advice. The content within this book has been derived from various sources. Please consult a licensed professional before attempting any techniques outlined in this book.

By reading this document, the reader agrees that under no circumstances is the author responsible for any losses, direct or indirect, which are incurred as a result of the use of information contained within this document, including, but not limited to, — errors, omissions, or inaccuracies

Table Of Contents

Introduction 4

Chapter 1: Lala's Crooked Unicorn Horn 6

Chapter 2: Every Shiny Thing 11

Chapter 3: The True Tale of Atlantis 18

Chapter 4: A Mermaid's Song 37

Chapter 5: If Trees Can Cry 45

Chapter 6: Hot Hot Hot! 49

Chapter 7: How Angels Get Wings 55

Chapter 8: A Tattletale Parrot 59

Chapter 9: The Rooster's Crow 63

Chapter 10: Pia's First Day 65

Chapter 11: Picky-eater Nana 68

Chapter 12: Art of Sorry 71

Chapter 13: The Fairest of Them All 74

Chapter 14: Falling From Grace 82

Chapter 15: Tiah's Sweets 87

Chapter 16: Royal Double Trouble 98

Conclusion 103

Thank you 104

Introduction

This book contains new spins to old folktales found in different parts of the world.

Even in the past, stories, legends, and tales were used to teach children how to love themselves and other people around them. Fairytales can ignite the artistic and creative side of children. They are wondrous storytellers if only we would care to listen to them. They can imagine a world that adults can't even grasp. We can look into the heart of a child and pluck out a story or two. Let us listen to a few to reflect on life and how beautiful the world is in the eyes of a child.

Courage is something children learn by failing and there must be many stories in the world talking about how a child can grow to be braver. The stories of legends and origins make the world more fantastical and inviting. By talking about how people in the past looked at the world, a child can learn about how times have changed from then to now.

Stories have a way of helping a child express themselves. Let them choose the story they want to hear and you can catch a glimpse of how they are feeling by bedtime. This book will provide various stories they can choose from.

There are re-imagined fairytales and modern twists to stories to make them more relatable to your child. As the world changes, so do stories. But the lessons they must teach our children remain the same. We must help them see the world as a beautiful place by letting them travel on story clouds. We can teach them how to love the planet with stories about critters they find adorable.

A child's mind is full of curiosity and tenacity to learn new things. They are always asking us the why's of the world. This book lets them hear those answers but with a dash of pixie dust thrown in.

We have fairytales, fantastical legends, and life lesson stories to entertain you and your child. We will move to Urania, a fantasy kingdom, where stories come to life and everything is magic. Pick one story or two to get them to sleep and they will be dreaming of those tales until morning.

Thanks for purchasing this book. I hope you enjoy it!

Chapter 1: Lala's Crooked Unicorn Horn

This is a story about a sweet young unicorn named Lala. She loves being with her mom and her dad while they run around in the cloud field of Urania. Their kingdom is full of all sorts of magical creatures. In other worlds, unicorns are a myth but in Urania, they are the noblest of steeds.

The first king of Urania became friends with Lala's great ancestor, Landor. Landor was the first unicorn in Urania. His beloved mate was Masha, a unicorn that came from another world. They fell in love and many unicorns came to be in Urania.

Lala was born in a beautiful spring evening and so her mother, Marisa, and her father, Lansel, loved their unicorn pony very much. She was the first pony born to her parents after many years of them being together.

Lala grew up in the loving care of her family and she never really felt any sadness. She didn't always get what she wanted but she was very much loved.

It was the first day to play with other unicorn ponies that brought her the first sadness in her life.

She was eager to make new friends but the other ponies didn't want to play with her. She went home before the moon came out and cried to her mother.

"No one wants to be my friend!"

"Don't worry, my lovely Lala. Tomorrow, you can try again."

Lala went to sleep early because she hoped that would make tomorrow come sooner.

The next day, the other ponies were still playing with each other and left Lala to play on her own. She was worried she did something wrong to them so she asked one of the other ponies, "Do you want to play with me?"

"I don't want to play with you. Your horn is wrong," the other pony said.

"My horn is not wrong, it's crooked! I was born with it." Lala showed off her slightly bent horn.

"Unicorn horns are long and straight. If your horn is wrong, then...you're not a unicorn! You're a ram or a goat!" Lala was surprised with what the other pony said.

She was born with a crooked horn but her family never said her horn was wrong. They always told her she was lovely every day. But the other ponies were calling out, "Lala has a crooked horn! Lala is a go-oooat!"

Chapter 1: Lala's Crooked Unicorn Horn

This time Lala went home but didn't tell her mother that she was crying. She lay on her fluffy hay bed and cried until she fell asleep. Chapter 1: Lala's Crooked Unicorn Horn

Lala had a dream that night; the unicorn mother Masha came to her dream. "Why are you crying, my lovely pony?"

"The other ponies don't want to be my friend because I am ugly."

"None of the creatures in Urania are ugly. We look different from each other, but everyone is beautiful."

"They said that my horn is wrong."

"Your horn is not wrong, it's different. It's okay to be different as long as you are still a good pony."

"Why won't they play with me then?"

"It's because they are not ready. Find the ponies who are ready to play with you and then the others would see you for you."

"See me for me?"

"You are a loving pony, are you not?"

"Yes, and I can run really fast."

"Show them. Don't be bothered by those who tell you that your horn is wrong. The way they look at other ponies is the wrong thing. Everyone is beautiful, remember that." Lala smiled at what Masha said.

"I will!"

"Have fun tomorrow, Lala."

"I definitely will!"

When Lala woke up, she felt ready to play. She went to the cloud fields where the other ponies were playing and she greeted each one with a smile. "You are looking lovely today!"

Some of them smiled at her greeting but others ignored her. One of the ponies that smiled at her was a charming unicorn pony named Sope.

Lala approached Sope and asked, "Do you want to play with me?"

"Can you run really fast?" Sope asked. "I like running fast but the others get tired easily."

"My father runs with me every day so I can run really fast," Lala boasted.

"Last one to the fairy tree has to get food for the winner!" Sope challenged Lala then started running. Lala ran right after Sope and reached the fairy tree first.

The other ponies ran behind. "Wow, Lala is really fast!"

She looked very beautiful as she ran towards the tall, pink-leaved fairy tree.

Chapter 1: Lala's Crooked Unicorn Horn

Lala was greeted by the neighing of other ponies who thought she was great. Lala felt happy that they wanted to play with her. Sope stayed close to her and they ran every day and grew close.

And so, Lala remembered what Masha told her. "It's okay to be different as long as you are still a good pony."

Sope became her best friend because she taught Lala that being different doesn't matter as long as you are ready to love yourself and let others love you.

Chapter 2: Every Shiny Thing

Princess Jina of Urania loved shiny things. She always wore her tiara, even in her sleep.

"My dear Jina, take your tiara off when you sleep," her mother, Queen Dana, asked her one night.

"I am still a princess when I sleep. Why can't I wear my tiara then?"

"You have to let your neck rest from carrying the extra weight," her mother explained.

"I don't want to take it off! I will wear it every day."

The princess loved not just her tiara but all the royal jewels. One day she was in the palace by herself. She sneaked into the royal chamber where her parents slept and went into the secret passage that led to the crown jewels storage room.

When she got there, she saw there were more jewels that she hasn't seen before. In the corner of her eyes, an emerald ring winked at her.

"Come and take me." She was pretty sure that ring was speaking to her.

Chapter 2: Every Shiny Thing

She wore the gold ring that had the biggest emerald on it. "You are very lovely."

She knew she had to leave the ring behind because she wasn't even supposed to be in that room all by herself. "Take me with you." The whisper in her ear made her believe she could take it with her. "You are a princess. All of the jewels are yours because you are the daughter of the king and queen."

"That's right. You belong to me." She looked at the ring on her right ring finger. "Even Mother would not ask me about you if I took you."

Jina went back to her room with the ring glittering on her finger.

That supper, the royal protector whispered something to the king. "There has been a theft in the crown jewels room. An emerald ring was stolen." The king became angry and told the royal guards to look for the person who stole from the Royal family.

"Find that thief at once. That person needs to return it, or a curse will plague our kingdom!"

Jina was confused. *Why would getting one ring from that room cause a curse?*

"The first king had brought various riches from his world, but he feared that people would soon take from them what he had brought with him. A powerful magician placed the curse on the crown jewels. Should anyone, from Urania or other worlds, come to try to take what is his and his children's, then a curse will come upon them."

Jina was starting to feel itchy. She tried to remove the ring to remove the curse but it wouldn't budge.

"Father, my king, I have done something very bad." She showed the ring to her father and the royal couple was sad and disappointed.

"Why would you take something when you already have so much?" Her mother was worried about her and why she was doing that.

"It was the wrong thing to do. I am really sorry."

"Being sorry and solving the problem we have are two different things." The King called in a historian.

"You asked for me, Your Royal Highness?" A young historian came into the room.

"Where is master Ba, Arell?" The king was looking for the chief historian. The young historian who came was his son.

"My father sent me to take care of the matter. There was too much work that got piled up. We are catching up on all of them," Arell explained politely.

"Tell me what to do when the curse of the crown jewels starts happening?"

Chapter 2: Every Shiny Thing

"The curse can get lifted once someone pure of heart takes the ring off the princess' finger," Arell explained.

"That's easy then, we can ask anyone to take it off. Children are all pure of heart anyway." The queen was happy the solution was so easy.

"The person must not be a child, but a full-grown man." Jina had never met men apart from palace guards and her father. And giving her hand to another man means marriage in the kingdom of Urania.

"If you cannot do this, then the kingdom would start getting many different problems," the young historian told Princess Jina.

"Fine, let's do it." And so, a grand announcement was made across the kingdom. All young male royals were asked to come to the palace to receive the princess' favor. When she chooses that man, he would be a future king.

Many men from different kingdoms and worlds came to meet Princes Jina.

All the men who came to the palace on that day tried to take the emerald ring from Princess Jina's finger. They were all asked to bring a ring to signify their intent to marry the princess. But since none of the royals who came during the first day were able to remove the ring, the king and queen said all men, regardless of status and birthright, can ask for the princess' hand. It was to be done in a month's time.

The towns and cities were emptied of eligible men and they all traveled to the kingdom of Urania. Princess Jina was feeling more and more afraid. The lands around their kingdom had started to darken. The unicorns were getting sick. The people in the towns around the castle were experiencing severe drought.

On the day of the royal asking, the fish in the river floated into the surface. The rotten fish smell greeted all the bachelors as they traveled to the castle. The other men heard of the curse on the kingdom and thought the princess was the cause. The town folk spread the news that the reason why the princess was being asked to marry was to lift the curse.

"She must be unlucky to have been given away like this," one of the men said to another. "I came to be a king, not to fall in love with a princess. As soon as I get the throne, I can pick another queen when the one I have dies."

The young historian who knew of the truth was worried that Princess Jina would end up marrying one of the evil men who came to the kingdom. He served the crown and had the responsibility to write about what they did during their reign. Historians traditionally don't end up getting married because of the long hours they spend at the side of royalty.

Chapter 2: Every Shiny Thing

"I can't let her suffer just for one mistake." Arell looked at the young princess who was getting skinnier from all her sleepless nights.

The young historian was named Arell because his father chose a name that meant *light*. The chief historian wanted his son to continue to shine his light into the world full of darkness. Arell now wanted to be the light in Princess Jina's life.

During the royal asking, so many men came that Princess Jina was exhausted by the time the evening bells rang. There were still so many more suitors who had come to try to pull the ring from her finger. She was surprised to see Arell in front of her. "Are you not supposed to be writing about what is happening?"

"Today, I wish to be part of history instead." Arell read the book that held the story about the curse. It was a protection spell that would allow only someone who didn't covet the crown jewels to take the jewelry off the person who took one.

Arell pulled the ring off slowly and put a jade ring on the princess' finger. "My Princess Jina, I hope you remember never to take what is not yours. Not every shiny thing in the palace is for a princess'. But my heart is yours if you would have it."

Princess Jina was grateful the ring was taken back to the protected room. The king of Urania stood up and made an important announcement.

"We are grateful for your help in trying to lift the curse in our kingdom. Today is a joyous occasion and we invite all to celebrate the union of Princess Jina and Arell of Urania!"

Arell held Princess Jina's hand and smiled at her.

"Don't ever let me go. I hope you can continue to guide me, historian." Princess Jina looked at the clear eyes of the man she was supposed to wed.

"As long as you don't get the whole kingdom in trouble again, Princess." Arell winked at Princess Jina and the young princess laughed.

The many days of King Arell and Queen Jina paved way to the most magical of days in Urania. They had ten beautiful children who came to be known in all the realms as the "Gorgeous Troublemakers of Urania."

When asked, the king would simply look at his beloved queen and say, "An apple tree cannot bear peaches, after all."

Chapter 3: The True Tale of Atlantis

Many years ago, there was a beautiful and powerful city near the ocean called Atlantis. The people in that city lived in beautiful houses and learned many things about the world. One day a young apprentice named Zosimus found a door to another world. The door looked like a water mirror and he bravely walked through it.

The door was a magical door that a magician made in Urania. He cast a spell that linked Urania to Atlantis. The young man opened the door through accidental magic and that led him to a whole new world.

The magician, now very old, sat in a hammock near the door. He had seen in his dream the night before that someone would come through the door to deliver the news to the other world.

"Welcome, traveler," the old man greeted the newcomer.

"What place is this?" The young man looked around in awe.

"You are in Urania, land of the eternal," the old man explained.

The young man looked around and tried to get used to what he was seeing. The trees were not green but peach-colored, like the leaves were petals from cherry blossom trees. The grass was blue and the air felt warm but comforting. A bird flew above him and then circled over the old man. The old man stretched out his right hand, which was holding a long stick, and the bird landed on his arm.

"You're on fire!" The bird had a tail that was blue fire! The old man could catch fire! Blue is the hottest kind of fire after all!

"There are many creatures in Urania that are no longer found in your world. You might find those you only heard of in stories exist in our kingdom." The old man tried to ease Zosimus' mind.

The young man turned around, hoping the magical door was still there, but it was not. "How can I go back?"

"You can't. The door only opens from Atlantis' side." The old man's answer terrified the young Zosimus.

"How do you know of Atlantis?" Zosimus thought no one on the other side would know about his home.

"I am Minele, a magus here in Urania. I used to serve the king but I am now resting." The old man started walked towards a small house, so the young man followed him.

"My name is Zosimus, son of Vasilis." Zosimus decided it was best not to tell the old man about his status in Atlantis.

Chapter 3: The True Tale of Atlantis

He was afraid Minele would use his powers to keep Zosimus from leaving.

"And what do you do in Atlantis, young Zosimus?" The older man sounded curious.

"I am an apprentice. I learn from masters in the city. I learned from a healer, a trader, a ship captain, a farmer, and now I am learning from a builder."

"You must love to learn things." The old man opened his home to Zosimus.

"My father wants me to learn how the people built our kingdom. He says the past kings had made the people unhappy. A future leader must have the heart of the people." Zosimus looked around the hut and saw many uncanny things. There were shiny liquids in glass bottles but unlike the healer's bottles, the liquid inside looked alive.

"Well then, Prince Zosimus, have you ever been an apprentice of a magus?" Minele asked the young prince.

"I didn't say I was a prince." Zosimus was alarmed that Minele knew he was a prince.

"If your father is the king, then you are a prince. Are you not?" Minele's left eyebrow shot up.

"I am but…" Zosimus was not sure if he could tell Minele his secret.

"You are not born from the queen?" The young prince wondered if magus can read minds in Urania.

"Yes. I am only...half royalty." Zosimus was always insecure about the fact that he was not a full-blooded prince.

"Whatever half you are, in Urania none of that matters." Minele tried to comfort the prince.

"Can I really not go home?" Zosimus was torn between his curiosity of this world and his duties to Atlantis and his father.

"You can." The young man breathed a sigh of relief.

"How?" he asked, hopeful he could come back quickly.

"You must learn magic in order to open the door from this side." The answer he got was not that easy.

"You are a magus, can you not do it?" It would take him years to learn magic! He had to come back or his father might think he left Atlantis for good.

"My magic has weakened as I am nearing the end of my life. You must learn it so you can unlock the door from Urania's side. Then you can go and do your mission before it is too late."

Minele's last sentence bothered Zosimus. "Too late for what?"

Chapter 3: The True Tale of Atlantis

"That is a secret I cannot tell you now, when you don't have an ounce of magic in you. When it's the right time, you will learn of what the fate of your Atlantis would be." Zosimus became even more anxious.

"You make it sound like something bad will happen." He found the motivation to go back home. Whatever it was that was coming to Atlantis, he must stop it.

"All beginnings have an ending. That is the way of all the worlds. Your kingdom would fall if the person in the throne is a weak king. You must save your people from such a fate, Prince."

###

Zosimus started learning magic from Minele and the days passed in Urania without much trouble. One day, a young lady came running through the field and hugged Zosimus from behind.

"Minele, I missed you!" Zosimus turned around and was surprised to see a beautiful woman with green hair. She looked like a siren from the stories the royal storyteller talked about.

"Oh, I am very sorry. I thought you were Minele." The young lady bowed deeply and smiled at Zosimus. He felt like someone punched his chest, he could barely breathe. She was so beautiful.

"I'm Mara, what's your name?"

"I'm Zosimus, son of Vasilis." He bowed at the young woman out of habit.

"What kind of creature are you?" Her face was too close to Zosimus' own that it made his cheeks hot.

"I am a man." Zosimus was confused with her question.

"I see." Mara looked at him with an even more curious stare.

"And how about you? Are you a fairy?" Zosimus wouldn't be surprised if she was an angel.

"Me, a fairy? I wish! I am a human too." He couldn't believe it, how could a woman be so beautiful?

"Princess Mara, what brings you to my humble home?" Minele greeted Mara from the door.

"Minele!" Mara ran into the old man's arms and laughed happily. Zosimus was filled with warmth with the sound of her laughter.

"Thank you for traveling to my home. My old bones don't allow me to come to the palace to see you."

"Father could just come here but he is too busy with so many things." Mara pouted.

Chapter 3: The True Tale of Atlantis

"He is king. Why would the king come to see an old magus?" Minele laughed at Mara's cuteness.

"You're a legendary magus who helped my parents help the whole kingdom. If not for your help, so many of our people would have died!" Zosimus knew that Minele was a wise magus but the young man didn't know he was legendary.

"You are still not telling me why you are here," Minele asked her.

"I dreamt of a bad thing and I wanted to ask you about it. Father told me I could not go alone. But it was too scary that I had to talk to you immediately." Mara almost said everything in one breath.

Minele shook his head. "And so you ran away without a guard?"

"Perhaps," Mara smiled, caught in her lie.

The sound of hooves made them all look at the incoming guards. With them was a white horse that reminded Zosimus of a legendary winged unicorn in Greek myths.

Minele bowed deeply and Zosimus followed suit. "I am honored by your visit, Your Majesty."

"You can thank the princess for this visit, Minele." There was steel behind the voice of the king that made Mara make a small whimpering sound.

The king got off the winged unicorn and faced the princess and Minele. "Let's go inside to talk about why you had to come here unguarded."

All four of them went inside while the royal guards waited outside. The king looked around the house and had a small smile on his face. "I miss this place more than I miss any other."

"Did you come to visit here often, Your Majesty?" Zosimus couldn't help but ask. The king looked at him as if he was trying to remember who he was. "I am Zosimus, son of Vasilis. I am from Atlantis."

"He is from that cursed place? Why did you bring him here?" The king suddenly turned to Minele in anger.

"King Arell, he is Prince Zosimus, son of King Vasilis of Atlantis." Minele introduced Zosimus properly. "He came here to be my apprentice, just as you were when you were his age."

"This changes nothing. He is not from here so bring him back to his own world." King Arell wanted Zosimus gone as soon as possible.

"I cannot for I am too weak to open the gate." Minele told the king the real reason why the young man was still in Urania.

Chapter 3: The True Tale of Atlantis

"I will ask the royal magi to help you." King Arell's face was stern but his eyes were full of fear. He faced Zosimus and said, "You do not belong in this kingdom. You have to go back and fix your own world."

"Would you not help him, Father?" Mara asked King Arell.

"I am not their king. Vasilis is their king. He should take care of his own kingdom." The bitterness in the voice of the king could not be mistaken.

"But he was your friend." Minele spoke so softly that Zosimus barely heard it.

"You knew my father?" Zosimus swore he would have known from his mother if she was friends with another king.

"Our king was a historian in the palace but he was a magus in training once. When he managed to open a door to the other world, he went through it and was lost in the city of Atlantis where he met a young man named Vasilis," Minele told Zosimus.

"That story is wrong. I met a young lady named Elipda who helped me learn how to survive in Atlantis. I met Vasilis because of her." King Arell sighed. "How I wish I had not met him."

"My mother's name is Elipda." Zosimus felt like he was not being told a part of the story.

"Your mother was a warrior and your father fell in love with her. I left Atlantis and began my work in the palace to forget my time in your kingdom." Mara was by her father's side and was trying to comfort the worried king.

"You don't have to forget memories if they are not painful. You have to love a place in order for good memories to be painful." Mara's words made the king sit down and look out the window.

"Father, my dream was that Atlantis was underwater." Mara asked his father an important question, "Zosimus said he is a man. Can men in Atlantis breathe underwater?"

"No, we can't." Zosimus was alarmed by Mara's story. "Is the princess a seer?" Minele nodded when the young man asked.

"Father, we must help the people! If I see something like that, usually it happens pretty soon." Mara was panicking.

"Atlantis is protected by Poseidon. He would never let the city fall, let alone drown." King Arell knew as much.

Minele sat in front of the king, who tried to look away. The old man held the king's hands and said, "You have a queen, ten beautiful daughters, and a kingdom that is thriving. Vasilis has become darker than the last time you met him. He had tried to expand his kingdom, thinking that if he did that he would make up for not being a king of a magical kingdom. Be the better king and help the people of Atlantis."

Chapter 3: The True Tale of Atlantis

King Arell stood up and faced Zosimus. "Come back to Atlantis. Tell your mother that divine punishment is coming to Atlantis. You must bring as many of your people through to Urania. We will open the gate wider for ten days. All those who do not go through will live through what Mara dreamt about."

"If you know this, why didn't you tell my father? He was a prince then. He could have prevented this." Zosimus' mind was full of thoughts of what could happen.

"I told your mother but your father never believed that I was from Urania. He only saw me as a poor apprentice who didn't know much of your world. I don't blame him for thinking I am a fool. But you were sent here by your god as a way to protect the people whom he loved. Bring your people here and I will give you refuge as your mother had done for me."

"But I can't open the door yet. I am not strong enough." Zosimus was afraid he couldn't do it.

King Arell put his hands on Zosimus' shoulders. "Two apprentice magi and a teacher can do it, don't you think so?" Minele nodded at the king's suggestion.

"Many thanks, Your Majesty. Our kingdom would be forever in your debt." Zosimus had tears in his eyes from relief.

"It is you who are helping me pay back my debt to your mother." King Arell was smiling at Zosimus. "You are brave, just like your mother."

King Arell, Zosimus, and Minele came outside after the young man packed what he needed for his trip back. King Arell gave him an arrow tip tied on a leather string. "Your mother gave me this when I first came to Atlantis. She would remember me and believe you when she sees it."

The three of them closed their eyes and began to say the spell that opens the door to the other world. Mara prayed for the door to open too.

When the water mirror door opened Mara cheered happily. She gave a small token to Zosimus. "This is a siren's tear. It can help heal any kind of ill. Use it only when you really need to."

"This is a precious thing to give to someone you just met." Zosimus was honored to receive such a gift from the princess.

"You are a hero who needs many weapons to save your people. My sister gave me that tear for me to use. I can get another one from our siren friends." Mara tried to hide her blushing.

Minele leaned over to whisper to King Arell. "Perhaps your story would have a different ending for them."

Chapter 3: The True Tale of Atlantis

"I wish for nothing but to have Mara find a good man to love. She is the most adventurous of my daughters." King Arell hoped for the best.

"It's because Mara is gifted; that is why she is exceptionally brave," Minele explained.

"Sometimes I wish she didn't get that gift from me." The gift of sight was always a heavy burden to carry.

"And her reckless nature from her mother." Minele laughed at the memory of Queen Jina during her youthful days.

"Apple trees cannot bear peaches, after all." The two older men laughed at the memory of the reckless princess days of Queen Jina.

Zosimus kissed the back of Mara's hand and bowed to the king and Minele to say goodbye.

"Come back safely, Prince Zosimus," Mara said with a smile.

"Your wish is my command, Princess Mara." And with that, Zosimus went through the door. He found himself in the middle of the market place in Atlantis. He rushed to the palace and met with his mother.

"Where have you been, my child? I have been so worried!" His mother hugged him for what felt like ages before she started showering him with questions.

"Mother, I met Arell. He told me to give you this." He took out the arrowhead pendant.

Lady Elipda gasped and began to cry. "He made it back home! I am so glad."

"There is more. He gave me a message that I must tell Father." Zosimus felt anxious. He didn't know how to begin to tell his mother what was to come.

"Is it about the drowning of Atlantis?" His mother sat him down and clasped his hands. "I have been trying to tell your father that it is coming but he doesn't believe me. He thinks if the kingdom has more land then we would be safe."

"He can't be king if his kingdom's capital drowns." Zosimus knew this and his mother was just as worried. "We must save our people. King Arell told me he would keep the gate open for ten days. It's all the time we have."

"I will ask your father to talk to his ministers about it. But I do not think anyone would want to believe that Urania exists. They have never even heard of it." Lady Elipda knew the ministers would be hard to convince. She has been trying to get many of them on her side for years. But to this day only a handful are willing to honor her.

"Mother, I am the proof. I was there. I learned magic there from Minele, a magus. I met Arell. He is the king there. His daughter has the same gift and she dreamt of Atlantis being underwater. She gave me this." Zosimus showed her the vial that had the siren's tear. "It's a siren's tear. It can cure any

Chapter 3: The True Tale of Atlantis

illness. Mother please, we need to save Atlanteans from what is coming."

"I will do my best to get you an audience in the Hall of Honors. You can talk to the ministers yourself. If they believe you, then we will prepare to move the people. If there is no one who wants to believe you, we will gather those who want to leave with us. I am going with you." His mother was a warrior once and she had friends who would follow her to Hades if she so asks.

"You are not scared, are you?" Zosimus teased his mother.

"I'm not scared, just very worried. Arell is my brother, after all," Elipda replied.

"I don't think Father likes him very much. He never mentioned him to us. You never mentioned him to me either." Zosimus hardly spent time in the king's presence.

"Your father is a good man but he is not without his pride. He feels like Arell was too arrogant and rude sometimes." Elipda has spent her life trying to reunite the two brothers.

"Mother, we have no time. Talk to Father and I will go and fetch your brothers first." Zosimus was talking about his mother's battle comrades. They had fought wars together and now were living outside the palace in a small farm off the capitol.

When he arrived there, they were happy to see them. He told them of his meeting with Minele, Arell, and Mara. "You must want to come back because of that princess," one of them teased him.

"It's not entirely because of her. It's also because Atlantis will be under water soon." They all looked like they have heard the story before.

"Arell used to tell us that he dreamt of Atlantis befalling such a fate. But it has been two decades since he left and there hasn't been a single flood in Atlantis." The oldest of the group, Archan, didn't seem all that convinced.

"My mother wishes to go to Urania with all her brothers. If you believe in her words, then you will come with me and see for yourselves." Because of what Zosimus said, the old soldiers went with him to the gateway.

"Arell, you have gotten older!" Archan tried to march to King Arell to hug the king but the guards stopped him.

"Let him pass. He is my brother." Archan was then able to hug the king. The rest of the men greeted the king like he was one of them.

"It's been too long, my brothers. Where is Elipda?" the king asked.

"She is trying to convince my father to leave the city and come here." Zosimus told Arell.

Chapter 3: The True Tale of Atlantis

"She is in danger then." Arell's face was pale as parchment. "If she tries to talk to that man, he might strike her down."

Zosimus ran back into the gateway. Archan ordered the men to stay in Urania. "I'll follow the prince."

"Leader, we must bring the people here." The youngest of them knew the king would not change his heart.

Archan sighed and then nodded. "Bring as many of your kin to this side. Bring only people so you can travel light."

"We can provide whatever the people might need. So come quickly and safely through the gates. Even the seers do not know when the water will come," Arell told the other soldiers. They ran back into the gateway. Shortly, old men, women, and children were walking through the gateway. King Arell had ordered for carriages to come to the field to bring the newcomers to the palace. The princesses were helping the Atlanteans get used to the new place.

"We simply told the townsfolk that a war was breaking out. We didn't tell them of what else was to come. It was easier to tell them that than the truth." The young soldier told King Arell, who seemed to agree with the white lie.

Mara came to the king's side. "Father, we must hurry. The gods have decided that today is when Atlantis falls."

The other people who just arrived heard what the princess said and they panicked. "My husband has stayed to fight. I can't live if he dies!" The panic spread among the others. Mara bit her lower lip in guilt.

"Find the prince and Elipda. Do not stop for anything else! They must come through before we get anyone else." King Arell was panicking too. The soldiers followed his orders.

Wet and distraught, Zosimus came through the gateway. "I'm back." He fainted in Mara's arms.

The other soldiers were also wet and crying; some were on their backs from exhaustion. Minele closed the gateway behind them. The water was visible through the closed gateway. The fate of Atlantis had come upon the kingdom.

When Zosimus woke up, he told the soldiers and King Arell what became of his family. "My father was upset that my mother was talking about Urania again. The queen had ordered for my mother to be sent to the deepest dungeon. I tried to bargain with my father. I told him I would leave with my mother and never come back. The queen let me take her. I had begged for them to come to the gateway with me. Atlantis could start over if the royal family was still together. My brothers and sisters only laughed at me when I told them about what Mara said."

Mara hugged him to comfort him. "My mother and I were coming back when the water surged from the ocean into the streets. We were a few feet from the gateway when the water caught my mother and she was pulled back into the ocean. I

Chapter 3: The True Tale of Atlantis

saw the water take the people, carriages, and even parts of the houses back into the ocean."

"Sometimes the gods of your world are too cruel." King Arell was crying for his lost friends.

"All is not lost." Zosimus looked around the room and saw the faces of his mother's comrades. "Poseidon told me before he pushed me through the gateway that we must keep our people in our hearts. We might have lost our home but Atlantis is not an island, it is the people. As long as we are together, we can rebuild our home anywhere."

And so the tale of Atlantis became myth in the other world but in Urania, it is a small city where unique men and women live. They speak in a language different from those that Uranians can speak but they have learned the language of the new land, of the fairies, and even those of the merfolk.

Zosimus, their new leader, later became a prince of Urania when he married Princess Mara. King Arell is teaching the young prince all that he knows, hoping that someday he will take a seat in the king's court of advisers.

No tale truly ends in tragedy. There are always those who survive and start a new tale.

Chapter 4: A Mermaid's Song

The sea of Urania has a secret passage that leads to the big ocean in the other world. Marina is a mermaid who has a cousin, Coralina, who lives on the other side.

One day, Marina decided to visit her cousin Coralina in the big ocean. She remembered there were many fish and colorful corals in the big ocean.

When she passed the cave passage she was surprised to see many floating things in the water. It tasted different too. It wasn't easy to breathe and there was oil sticking to her skin. It made her skin itchy and she couldn't see well in front of her.

She took out the big shell Coralina gave to her. She blew on it to call for her cousin. She waited and waited but Coralina did not come.

She was all alone in the dark and dirty ocean. She was about to go home to Urania's green sea when she heard someone calling for help.

"Please help me, anyone. Please, I'm stuck!" She swam towards the voice and saw a turtle with something wrapped around its neck.

Chapter 4: A Mermaid's Song

"Master Turtle, what is that on your neck?" Marina asked.

"It's plastic. I was swimming and could not see it. My head went through the circle but my body could not. Now it's stuck on my neck like a necklace. Help me take it off." Marina didn't know what *plastic* was. They did not have such things in Urania. But she had a feeling it might be a bad thing because it was attacking turtles.

She tried to cut the plastic with a sharp flat rock she had with her. The turtle had a red mark on its neck after the plastic was removed. "Master Turtle, is plastic a bad creature that lives in the big ocean?"

"It's not alive. It's trash. Don't you know what plastic is?" The turtle seemed surprised that she did not know.

"I'm sorry, Master Turtle. I am Marina from Urania. I live in the Green Sea. I don't live in these waters."

"Well, all the merfolk left these waters last year. They had to leave because they kept getting hurt and people kept throwing trash into the ocean. The waves bring them from islands, big and small. They couldn't stop them anymore."

"That's so bad. Why are people throwing evil things into the ocean?"

"The plastic is not evil. It's just a thing people made. But many fish eat them because they think they are jellyfish.

Before they know it, they are sick for eating the wrong thing."

"Master Turtle, where are the merfolk now?"

"They are in the big hidden cove that can't be reached by humans. But I don't know who can help you find them. They must have left some markers but you can't see them in these dark waters."

"I have to find my cousin and help her go to Urania. The big ocean is not good for mermaids anymore."

"When the merfolk finally leave, then the whole ocean will die. That's why they are staying even if it is dangerous for them."

"Why didn't Coralina tell me what was happening?" Marina always told Coralina her problems through the magical mirror they shared. She was hurt that Coralina never asked her for help.

"Coralina? She is not here." The turtle looked concerned. "She came to the surface to tell the people to stop putting trash into the big ocean. She hasn't been back in years."

Marina took out her magical mirror and tried to reach Coralina. "Coralina, come and talk to me."

"Marina! How are you?" Coralina greeted her sweetly.

"Where are you right now?" Marina frowned.

Chapter 4: A Mermaid's Song

"I am in the big ocean, silly. Where else would I be?" Coralina laughed nervously.

"Master Turtle said you are in the surface!"

Coralina looked shocked. "Are you in the big ocean right now? No, Marina! You should go home. It's not safe in the big ocean!"

"I saw it. I saved a turtle from that evil plastic." Marina was really angry. "Why are you in the surface? Do you want to become bubbles too?" There was a sad story about a mermaid who became bubbles. They were not allowed to go to the surface at all.

"I have to come here. People are destroying our home. They don't listen to our kind because they think mermaids are story characters. In Urania it's different. Your king is wise and good. Here, the kings worship gold."

"I'll come and help you." Marina knew that Coralina would do things that were dangerous if she was all alone.

"It's too hard to pretend to be human, Marina. You don't have to come. It's my ocean to protect."

"I am going to help you because I want to see the big ocean be clean again."

Marina went to the surface and took out a pearl necklace her mother gave to her. She was to use it only when she had to go to the surface during a storm. But now she was using it to become a human. She swallowed and said, "To a human." Her beautiful pink tail became legs. It was hard to walk for a few steps but when she got used to it, she skipped and ran.

"What a wonderful feeling, sand on my feet and the sky in my hands." The sky was something she always longed to see. Even in Urania, it was hard for her to come to the surface to take a look. Now, she was going to help Coralina and also see the sky as much as she could.

Coralina was waiting for her near the breakwater. "Marina, you really came!"

"I always do what I promise to do." The two mermaids hugged each other. "I have missed you so much."

"I have missed you a lot too." Coralina looked like a mermaid even in her human clothes. She had black flowing hair and her dress was shiny like scales. "You can take the mermaid out of the big ocean but you can't take her scales off." Coralina laughed and showed off her clothes. "I was supposed to be doing a show for children when you called for me. I had to come to you or you would have been as lost as I was when I first came here."

"You are lucky a fisherman didn't catch you!"

Coralina smiled and hugged her cousin some more. "I was lucky. A boat of big ocean lovers found me and helped me with my goal."

Chapter 4: A Mermaid's Song

"What is your goal anyway?" Marina knew mermaids had magic that could control people but outside of the water, that power was weaker.

"I helped take videos of the bad things that happened in the big ocean. I can go to places where people can't normally go. This way, we are able to show the people just how bad the situation is."

"Why didn't you just go to the cove with the others?"

"I am not afraid to do something that can help us all. I won't be happy just praying to the ocean god for protection." Coralina was always a fighter. She does everything very well and does what she thinks is best for everyone.

"How can I help you?" Coralina looked like she was thinking very hard.

"You can sing!" Marina did love singing but it was always just to her family. She never sang in front of strangers.

"I am not sure if people would like my singing here." Coralina took out something from her bag.

"This is called a video camera. We can take a video of your singing and people can watch it and be inspired to help. We can sing the songs we sing in the big ocean and in Urania!"

"Would people like those songs?" Marina didn't know if humans like merfolk songs.

"Our songs are about the beauty of the ocean and the creatures that live in the water. It's a world they don't know but if we sing about it, they can come to care for it more." Coralina was very excited.

Marina began to sing and Coralina took a video of it. Many people heard Marina sing that day. They stopped in the beach and took out their cameras and mobile phones. Marina's song was about Master Turtle's painful encounter with plastic.

People clapped after hearing her song. Coralina was very happy. "Do you really think my song can help?"

"Every little thing can help. If we can tell one person about how beautiful the ocean and the creatures living in it are, then that is one less person who would throw bad things into the ocean."

Marina looked at the big ocean and heard the waves crying. "The big ocean is asking for us to help it. She feels like she has so many things she has to carry."

"I listen to the ocean every day too. I just hope someday, she can sing happy songs again." Coralina smiled a sad smile.

"Humans are gifted with so many things. I hope they learn that the ocean is someone's home too."

Chapter 4: A Mermaid's Song

"Now *that* is something we can sing about!" Coralina and Marina looked at the ocean and prayed for the day when the ocean can sing happy songs again.

Chapter 5: If Trees Can Cry

Summer was unusually hot in Urania that year. King Arell was worried about the forest that was getting hotter and hotter each day.

Queen Jina came in a rush one day and said, "The forest is on fire!"

The king and queen looked out from the castle balcony and saw something red in the horizon. Only it was not the sun setting, it was trees on fire. The black smoke that was rising up was a sign that it was not about to stop.

"Call the water fairies and the forest nymphs! We have to stop the fire from spreading." King Arell barked orders to the guards and changed from his royal robes to lighter clothes.

"My queen, I have to go and help the forest folk kill the fire."

"Be careful. Take the magi with you." Magicians are able to make it rain so that would be very helpful.

The water fairies made water flow from the rivers and the ocean, and formed clouds. The magicians made it rain heavily over the forest. The forest nymphs looked for the animals trapped in the forest and took them to safety. They

Chapter 5: If Trees Can Cry

told the water fairies where embers were still alive in order to wash them all away.

By the end of the day, the wild fire was completely gone. There was a large part of the forest that was charred. The forest nymphs were too tired to urge the forest to heal.

King Arell thought of what they could do. "Bring me the man who started the fire."

The fire starter was a farmer who wanted to use a bit of the forest as his farmland. It was not allowed under the king's orders because the forest was home to the nymphs, trees, and animals. Fire had no master and could burn everything in its path.

"Speak your mind, farmer. Tell me how I should punish you." King Arell was well-known for being kind. He always asked the person who committed the crime to think of the best punishment. If he agrees then they are asked to carry out the punishment. If he does not agree, he gives them just the right amount of penance to do.

"I did not know one fire could cause so much damage. I do not think my life is enough to pay for all that was lost because of my selfishness." The farmer was bowing down on the ground.

"If your life is not enough, then many lives must be used as payment." The man looked scared. He thought the king would ask for many human lives instead. "Hear me, farmer! You are now going to give your life to bring back the forest to the wondrous place it used to be. Call for all farmers in the land to clear off the burned things and plant new trees in their place. Man, woman, and older children, each one must plant a tree to represent their life."

"Why must everyone do this?" The farmer was confused.

"Each tree will be linked to that human. Each life will be represented by this. If the tree grows well and is good, the human's life will be good. If the tree dies or burns, then the human's life will be bad."

The farmer did not know how he could tell people about this. "Worry not, farmer, for I will plant a tree myself. All of the people of Urania will come far and wide to plant a tree and we will regain our forest soon."

The king's royal decree was met with speculation. But because the king was beloved by his people, they all planted a tree. The years passed and each seedling grew into wondrous trees. The forest nymphs took care of each tree and the people of Urania began a new tradition. Every time a child is born, a tree is planted in the forest. For every life, a tree is planted.

The forest of Urania never caught fire again. Each man, woman, and child protected the trees because they were linked to them. Because of the love and support of the whole

Chapter 5: If Trees Can Cry

kingdom, the forest flourished and gave fruits, clean air, and a wonderful view. The creatures that lived in the forest were happy too.

In a world where a tree is as precious as a person, there is no forest that would ever be barren.

Chapter 6: Hot Hot Hot!

Pampam is a snow fairy who lives in Urania. She is learning to be a snow guide and was sent to her Auntie Tartica to train.

She passed through the glass mirror and arrived in the North Pole. Her Auntie Tartica was very happy to see her.

"Pampam, welcome to the North Pole!" Tartica hugged Pampam.

"Auntie Tartica, I am so happy to be here! The snow in Urania is very soft. Here we have more holy snow."

"The humans call it permafrost," Tartica was quick to teach her.

"And the sea mountains must be huge!"

"You mean the glaciers? Oh, why yes they are."

Pampam couldn't help but feel excited. The snow fluttered around her. "What is the first thing you are going to teach me, Auntie?"

Before Tartica could say anything, a snow pixie appeared in front of Pampam and her aunt.

"Lady Tartica, we have an emergency!"

Chapter 6: Hot Hot Hot!

"What's the problem, Lexa?" The snow pixie waved at the glass mirror nearby and showed Pampam and Tartica what the emergency was.

They saw a large piece of the ice breaking off from the large ice island. "Another piece broke away from the island! We can't stop the ice from melting!"

Tartica and Pampam flew together with Lexa to try to catch the breakaway glacial ice. "Auntie, why is the holy ice island falling apart? What dark magic is at work here?"

"This world is too hot," Lexa said with a sad voice. "It's the fault of the humans who made bad things that trapped the energy of their burning star."

"I don't understand."

"Humans call it global warming. It's not dark magic so we can't undo it in a snap. The problems it causes keep adding up. The pixies are dying out from exhaustion." Tartica was also very worried.

"If it's this bad, you should all just go to Urania. Our world can keep you safe. You don't have to live in this hot place!" Pampam didn't like knowing that snow pixies were getting hurt.

"We can't leave this place, Pampam. Our purpose is to protect the holy ice and the seasons. If we leave, no one would mind winter. This world would be thrown in eternal summer." Tartica knew that without the snow fairies, the balance of the seasons would be broken.

"Why are humans making all of these problems but not doing anything to stop the bad effects?" Pampam lived in a world where balance was very important. King Arell always made sure that Urania's creatures and beings were safe from bad things. The creatures made sure not to do anything that could harm others. The rest of them drive out any evil together.

"There are good humans who fight for their planet. They think of the future generations and wish to give them a chance to see nature." Lexa floated around Pampam's head. "But there are others who do not care about the future. They made things that poisoned the air, water, and land."

"What can we do? The water is rising and their world will be underwater." Pampam was near tears.

"We have to do what snow fairies are supposed to do." Tartica was firm.

"It's not enough! Look at that sky, there is a hole that is letting the burning star's heat. Nothing comes out and we are boiling in this place." Pampam held Lexa, who was crying in panic.

Tartica directed her freezing magic into the small glacial islet that was floating away. The water froze near it and

Chapter 6: Hot Hot Hot!

made the islet stay in place. Pampam pointed her freezing magic at the main ice island and together the two snow fairies connected the big island with the islet.

Tired from using so much magic, Tartica and Pampam changed forms and walked among the humans. "I need you to see that people are not as bad as Lexa thinks. There is hope."

"I don't see much of it here." Pampam was already feeling very hot.

"That is because you are not looking." Tartica led her to a bigger street where there were people gathered and shouting together.

"What are they shouting about?" Pampam asked.

"They are asking the leaders of their planet to protect it." Pampam didn't understand why they had to do that in the street. "Other people, who have the same goal, can see what they are doing and would join them. They become one voice that tries to tell the other humans that this place needs help."

"Those are just words. If they keep making things that will hurt their home, it's no use." Pampam felt doom was close because most of the people were not joining the big group who were chanting, "Save our planet! Save our home!"

"That is why they must teach the children." Tartica walked towards a park where there were tents and people.

"What are those things?" Pampam pointed at tall cups.

"People use it to drink water and other things. They made those so they don't have to use too many cups that get thrown away."

"Marina told me about the big ocean having those evil things called plastic. Are those things also evil plastic?"

Tartica laughed at Pampam's question. "Plastic is just a thing. How people use them is what makes the effect good or bad."

"Why make those unnatural things? In Urania we make things with wood or melted stone."

"They call that metal here. There are cups like that. Look over there." Tartica pointed at the metal tumblers. "Some people use metal cups and wooden things."

"Their king must remove all evil things that poison their water, air, and land."

"This place has no king."

"That explains why there is no order." Pampam shook her head.

"They have leaders and they do their best in trying to save their home. But the heart of the people must be reconnected

Chapter 6: Hot Hot Hot!

with their home in order for them to take better care of it." Tartica smiled as she explained to Pampam.

The younger snow fairy nodded. "I think I still have a lot to learn about how to help snow be loved by many."

"You came to the right place to learn that." Tartica waved her hand in the air and soft snow fell from the clouds.

People looked up and children cheered. "We just have to remind them that nature is something they can love, not use."

"Let's take it one snow day at a time." Pampam smiled at the people who were warming each other up by hugging and walking together under the snow.

Chapter 7: How Angels Get Wings

Princess Andera asked her father King Arell a very important question one day. "Father, how do angels get wings?"

The young princess was curious about many things. She asked questions every day. The king sat down next to the young princess and began the story. "In the other world, their god has magical warriors called angels. They were born from the love of that god and the wings are made from light."

"Can humans also become angels?" Andera asked.

"Yes, but they are not winged angels at first. They go to a place called Heaven and rest there. They have lived very difficult lives so they need to rest."

"But how come they don't have wings? Can they get wings later?" King Arell was sure Princess Andera was going to take after him. He also asked many questions when he was young.

"People who went to Heaven have their loved ones who are still living. Whenever a person prays for an unwinged angel, the prayer becomes light that can be turned into a feather."

Chapter 7: How Angels Get Wings

Andera looked very happy. She didn't like it that those angels did not have wings.

"Once they have enough feathers, they can fly down and do the mission their god asks of them."

"What kind of missions are those?" Andera was both curious and adventurous. King Arell knew she got it from Queen Jina. His wife was also a bit reckless when she was young.

"They bring messages to people about the world they live in. Sometimes there are messages for very special people. They must do a great deed or sacrifice in order to save the people."

"Do angels also visit kings in the other world?" Andera knew magical creatures and seers often visit her father.

"Why of course, kings are often visited by angels because their god used to choose the king of those people."

"Father, were you chosen by a god as well?"

King Arell nodded. "I believe so, yes. But there are no angels in Urania because we have many different creatures that are no longer living in the other world."

"I also want to go to Heaven and get wings, Father. Do I have to live in the other world to get wings?"

"I think the story goes like this. The god who grants wings made from light is a good king of Heaven. He accepts all those who love and help others. So if you grow up to be a good person who loves and helps others, when you die, your spirit will become an angel. Then the prayers of the people of Urania, who remember you when you were still alive, will become light and then wing feathers."

Andera was glad that even a princess in Urania could become an angel with wings. "What do I have to do to be a good princess who loves and helps others?"

"First, you must love your family and follow your mother and I well." Andera was worried because she often does whatever she wants. She fights with her sisters over small things.

"Then, you must learn to forgive those who have done bad things to you." Andera's eyes grew big.

"Even if they hurt me with their actions and words?" It didn't make sense to Andera that she should forgive those who hurt her.

"Even if they do. The god of the other world says that all the hurts and sacrifices will be paid back in Heaven with good feelings."

"Is there more?" Andera was thinking that the reason why angels are not common is because it was so hard to become one.

Chapter 7: How Angels Get Wings

"The last thing you must do is to help other people and creatures whenever they need help. Feed the hungry, clothe the poor, and care for the sick."

"Becoming an angel is harder than I thought." King Arell laughed at the worried princess.

"That is why they are granted their god's grace and can make miracles happen. What their god wills, they can do. Unlike fairies and magical creatures, their powers are limited only by their god's will."

"I want to gain wings so I should try my best."

"I shall look forward to you being a good girl." Andera locked pinky fingers with her father.

"I'll come and bring you messages when I become an angel too."

Chapter 8: A Tattletale Parrot

In Urania there was a famous little parrot named Lele. Lele was a beautiful rainbow-colored parrot with a golden beak. Many creatures marveled at Lele's beauty. But all the wonderful feathers in a bird could not make up for Lele's bad attitude.

For you see, Lele was known far and wide as the tattletale parrot. She talked about other creatures behind their backs, made up stories about other creatures, and even told humans about magical secrets.

"Did you know that sirens are singing near the rocks in order to make sailors crash against them?" Lele told one ship captain once and the story spread among the sailors of Urania.

The mermaids who tried to help the sailors during the storms were caught using fishnets. That's when Lele revealed the siren's true secret.

"Did you know mermaid tears become pearls?" Lele whispered into a greedy man's ear and the man went out to catch as many mermaids as he could. He hurt them to make many pearl necklaces.

Chapter 8: A Tattletale Parrot

The secret waterfall of the fairies was kept from humans. Lele told a woodsman about it. "If you take the bracelet of a fairy, she will have to become a human. If you marry her then she will bring you good fortune."

The woodsman took a fairy's bracelets and buried them. When the fairy became his wife, the woodsman became greedy and asked the fairy to make him rich.

Because the fairy was powerless without her bracelets, she could do no such thing.

The woodsman was angry and left the fairy in the middle of the woods by herself. He never returned the fairy's bracelets. She continued to wait for him to come back and return them.

Lele was so beautiful that even the princesses of Urania came to visit. Lele told the princesses what the woodsmen do, and they went home in tears.

Not long after, King Arell, King of Urania, heard of the bad things Lele was doing. "Lele of the North Forest, what say you about the stories you have told others?"

"Your Majesty, I bear no ill will. I was only making friends and sharing stories." King Arell could see Lele smile wickedly even though she was already caught.

"Do you know the words you shared with others hurt other creatures in Urania?" The king was a kind king who wanted to see the best in all of Uranians. He gave Lele one last chance to ask for forgiveness.

But Lele, blinded by the love of others who praised her feathers, refused to say she was sorry. "I did nothing wrong, Your Majesty. It is the human heart that used those stories for their selfish goals."

"Seeing that your pride does not let you take responsibility for your actions, I hereby banish you from Urania." King Arell asked the magi to open a door to the other world.

"In order to protect the humans and creatures of the other world from your poisonous words, you and your children will not be able to speak as freely as you can now. You can learn the words of those who protect you but only like an echo it shall be. You can't speak your mind or weave tales until your pride is gone, so shall be done." The head magus pointed a crooked staff at Lele. The green light hit the parrot and she began to squawk. No matter how hard she wanted to say something, she could only make sharp sounds.

Lele was released by a king's guard on the other side. The forest was hotter and there were many noisy birds around. Lele was still the most beautiful bird there but she felt lost because she could not let the others know what was on her mind.

She cried and her sadness took the color from her feathers. Her feathers became white and her beak that once was gold

Chapter 8: A Tattletale Parrot

was only now a few yellow feathers on her forehead. The brown beak she had was short and did not let her speak as many words as she wished.

She longed for the days when she could sing songs and marvel everyone with her feathers. She realized that bad deeds can lead one to an unhappy life. She taught her children what pride can do. Each one slowly learned how to speak words that humans used in that world.

The tale of Lele the tattletale parrot is spread far and wide in Urania. Every child, peasant or prince, learned how to tell the truth and to be trustworthy because of a rainbow-feathered parrot's tale.

Chapter 9: The Rooster's Crow

A farmer once owned a rooster who never crowed. A rooster that never crowed was a foul fowl.

"A rooster must crow, it's what you do!" The farmer was angry because the rooster remained quiet.

The rooster asked the hens, "Why do I have to crow? I like things to be quiet in the morning."

"A rooster must crow, it's what you do!" The hens went back to warming up the eggs in the henhouse.

"Why do I have to crow all day? It's not something I want. I want to play!" The thing the rooster hated to do was not just to crow but wake up early too.

"The sun can tell the time. When it's up, then it is planting time." The rooster was feeling blue; he didn't want to crow and bathe in the sun too.

The sun beat down on the rooster and said, "The farmer sleeps inside his home. Your crow is a reminder that I have come. Rooster, why do you hate crowing? How come? How come?"

"I like it quiet and I want to play. There must be more to being a rooster than crowing!"

Chapter 9: The Rooster's Crow

Little did the rooster know, the old farmer was thinking, *What's the use of a rooster besides crowing?*

The rooster heard the farmer tell his wife, "I shall let you make chicken soup if the rooster doesn't crow after tonight."

The rooster thought the hens were going to be eaten so the next morning he stood at the edge of the farm fence and faced the sun. He crowed for the first time in his life. The sound was small and did not reach the henhouse. The rooster tried again, and this time he crowed as loud as he could, "Be careful, don't be chicken soup!"

The hens heard the rooster and started to cluck, which woke up the farmer and his wife. "By golly, the rooster finally crowed!" The farmer's wife was delighted.

"And not a day too soon, or the rooster might have swam in the bottom of the pot." The farmer smiled at the rooster crowing with all its might.

Each day the rooster did his best, to warn the hens of becoming supper. Since that day, in all of the land, on the fence in every farm, roosters crowed.

Chapter 10: Pia's First Day

Princess Pia could not sleep that night. She closed her eyes but she could not fall asleep, for she was thinking of tomorrow.

Finally it was the first day of school!

Pia's older sisters were already in school, studying with other creatures and royals about how to live in Urania with others. She had prepared her ink stick, quills, parchment, and books. "I wonder if I can make new friends."

"Go to sleep, Pia. Tomorrow will be a full day for you." Queen Jina put Pia to sleep.

"School is going to be fun!" Princess Pia declared before she was tucked in.

###

The next day, Pia woke up early and had fairy pancakes for breakfast. She said goodbye to her father and mother and went to Fairy School with her older sisters.

There were creatures from all around Urania going to Fairy School that day. Pia was so excited and looked at every

Chapter 10: Pia's First Day

single thing in the road that she didn't see her big sisters go into their rooms.

Pia looked around her and everyone was already walking into their rooms. Pia didn't know where she was supposed to go. One of her sisters was supposed to walk her there.

She was about to cry when a summer pixie flew into her. "Aw, why are you in the way, giant?"

"I am not a giant. I am a princess." The back of Pia's head hurt because of the summer pixie.

"Oh, I am so sorry. I was in a hurry. It's my first day!"

"It's my first day too! I'm Pia, what's your name?"

The summer pixie twirled and said, "My name is Dilaw! I am a summer fairy who colors flowers."

"Oh, I love flowers! Let's be friends!" Pia and Dilaw walked to one of the rooms and was surprised to see a classroom of singing fairies. A siren was teaching an enchantment song to them.

"We are lost. Can you tell us where the first lessons are given?" Pia asked the siren.

"Oh, first class blues! The beginner class is in the next room. Good luck, Princess!" Pia thanked the teacher. Dilaw and Pia went to the next room.

###

"You're late!" A lovely leaf fairy was the teacher who greeted Pia and Dilaw next door. "Where have you two been?"

"I got left behind because I was looking at the wonderful woods." Pia felt shy because they were in front of the class.

"Hello, I am Dilaw. I am a summer fairy!"

"Welcome, Dilaw!" the class greeted her.

"I am Princess Pia, let's be friends!" Pia tried to get over her shyness by smiling at the class.

"Welcome, Princess Pia!" the class greeted her too.

Pia took the seat in front and Dilaw sat next to her. She played and learned about how leaves change color when the season changes. She was able to see how the moon looks when it wanes. There were many things she learned on her first day and she went home happy.

She told her mother and father about all the things she learned that day. Princess Pia made a new friend on her first day. She loved every new thing she learned. She went to school with a smile on her face each school day.

Chapter 11: Picky-eater Nana

"I don't want to eat veggies!" Princess Nana's loud scream echoed in the dining chamber. Queen Jina put down the fork with the carrot and asked Nana to eat it.

"Honey, carrots are good for you. They make your eyes see clearly." Nana shook her head.

"I don't want to eat veggies! They taste bad!" Nana tried to cry but the queen put the carrot down and faced Nana.

"You want to grow as tall and beautiful as your sisters, right love?" Nana nodded her head to say yes.

"Well, all of your sisters ate fruits and vegetables well."

"But why do veggies taste so bad?" Nana pouted.

"You have to try different kinds and find the ones you like. There are many vegetables and fruits that grow here. We can try them one by one. You can put butter on it, a little pepper, and eat it in cute spoonfuls."

Nana was still not sure. "Do I really have to eat them to be tall and strong?" Queen Jina nodded to answer yes to Princess Nana's question.

"There are a lot of foods that can make you tall and strong. You have to eat enough of them so you will grow up well." Queen Jina showed her the garden where the fruits and the vegetables were growing. "You might not like them all, but if you try just once, maybe you will."

"But some of them look like tiny trees. It's scary." Nana was trying to say no again.

"You can pretend that you are a giant who is eating a forest. A yummy, healthy forest!" Nana liked that idea.

Nana held a dragon fruit and said, "I am going to eat a dragon!"

Queen Jina laughed at Nana's announcement. "How about a hairy egg, Princess?" She showed Nana a kiwi. Nana looked at each fruit and vegetable and imagined that it was some magical creature.

"I am going to eat them all!" Nana growled like a monster. "Watch out veggies and fruits! Nanamonster is coming for you!"

Queen Jina was happy to see Nana was not afraid to try new things. Even if she sometimes said a vegetable is not to her liking, she was willing to try each at least once.

Princess Nana grew to be the guardian of the royal garden. She asked the young girls and boys to come and visit. The

Chapter 11: Picky-eater Nana

earlier they knew about veggies and fruits, the better. They could all be little giants gobbling up tiny forests of broccoli.

Chapter 12: Art of Sorry

Princess Meadow loved to play with her sisters' toys but she sometimes broke them.

One day she borrowed Princess Pia's doll and the arm came off. "Oh no! What should I do?" The pixie doll was made by Pia's best friend, the summer pixie Dilaw. It was her big sister's favorite toy.

"Oh, I know! I should hide it so she won't know I broke her toy!" She put the doll and the doll's arm in a wooden box and placed it under Princess Andera's bed.

When Princess Pia came to the room to ask Meadow about the pixie doll, Princess Meadow pretended to not know anything. "If you see my dolly, bring it to my room."

Princess Meadow was happy that Princess Pia didn't get angry at her. "I will. I'll make sure to bring you the doll when I see it."

Princess Pia looked for her doll in the whole castle. Even the King and the Queen helped. But no one could find it. Andera saw the box under her bed before bedtime and took it out.

"My pixie doll! Oh Andera, thank you for finding it!" Pia's happiness was short-lived when she saw the doll was

Chapter 12: Art of Sorry

missing an arm. "My dolly is broken! Her arm is missing!" Pia cried loudly.

Andera picked up the doll's arm from inside the box. "I found it too!"

"You broke my doll, Andera!" Pia was too angry and sad.

"No, I never played with your doll." The other princesses asked each other who broke the doll. Princess Meadow felt very bad that her sisters were fighting.

"I did it! I broke the doll. I'm sorry, big sister." Princess Meadow's cry made everyone go silent.

"I am so angry with you! You broke my dolly!" Princess Pia was crying hard too.

"But isn't it good that Meadow told us the truth?" King Arell asked Princess Pia, who slowly stopped crying. Pia looked at Meadow, who was crying very sadly.

"Meadow, it's okay. I am sure Dilaw's mother can fix my dolly." Pia tried to be brave and smiled at Meadow.

"I am really sorry I broke your doll, big sister." Meadow and Pia hugged each other.

"Let's make you another dolly and make sure to take care of them both!" Pia told Meadow.

"Yes! I promise to make sure that no dollies ever get hurt again!" Meadow pinkie promised with Pia.

The King and Queen smiled as they looked at their lovely daughters making up. "They can fight all day but always show love in the end. It's lovely," said the Queen.

"Family is more important than material things, after all," King Arell agreed.

Dilaw's mother fixed Pia's doll and made nine more for the other princesses. Now, the ten princesses played with their dolls every day until they were old enough to keep the lovely dolls in a special wooden box for their future princesses to play with.

"We should hide it under Andera's bed. She will be sure to remember when we need it." Pia smiled at Andera and the other princesses agreed.

In the castle of Urania, there is a special magical wooden box. Inside are ten dolls in the likeness of the princesses of Urania. It is said that if a young woman finds the doll, she could become a princess too.

Chapter 13: The Fairest of Them All

Princess Chalil was given a mirror for her eighteenth birthday. She loved looking at herself for most of her young life.

Many princes from different lands came to visit Urania to see the beautiful princesses.

At the age of eighteen, a princess is expected to find her one true pair. It means she either chooses someone she loves or the king is supposed to find a man worthy of the princess' love and hand in marriage.

"It is time to have a ball in your name, my lovely daughter." Queen Jina was very happy while preparing for her Chalil's birthday. But the young girl was not sure if there was anyone who she could love.

"You must look with your heart and not with your eyes. Our eyes can fool us. But our hearts always beats for the right one." Queen Jina knew this from experience. She was so happy to have met King Arell, even if it was through the help of a cursed emerald ring.

"Princes from different lands, worlds, and races would come to ask for your hand. Just like your father asked for mine. Only this time there would not be a curse to break."

"What if I don't have anyone whom I like?"

"There is a lid for every pot, Chalil. You would find your partner too. If the party is not enough, we can always wait for the deities to give you a message of whom to love and marry."

The day of the ball arrived and all manners of men and women were in the royal ballroom. The men who came to officially ask for Princess Chalil's hand in marriage reached a hundred. So each one was only given two minutes to talk to the princess. It was very hard on Chalil, as each one was either handsome or odd.

The ninety-ninth prince was done and the hall was waiting for the last prince to come up on the pedestal, but no one move from the crowd.

"I think the last prince was not able to come here. That is too bad." Queen Jina showed her dismay.

A loud sound startled everyone. It was the ballroom door opening loudly. "Sorry for being late!" A young man ran to the middle of the ballroom. His clothes were full of mud and his boots left a trail of boot prints on the pristine floor.

"You are very late, Prince Stellar." The queen didn't like latecomers.

Chapter 13: The Fairest of Them All

"I had to help with something on my way here, Your Majesty. My apologies to everyone—especially to you, dear Princess Chalil."

Chalil could barely hear his excuses because all she was focused on was his dirty state. When he came up to ask for her hand, she was reluctant to give it to him. It was so muddy and he smelled like earth.

"I am sorry for showing up like this in front of you, Your Royal Highness. I am beside myself for being this rude. But please know that I look like this because I had a good reason and because I had to make haste to make it to your side." Prince Stellar had a bright but apologetic smile on his face.

"Then tell us what it is then, your reason for being late."

"I made a promise not to tell what happened so I must say I'm sorry for not telling you the reason. It is not my secret to tell." Princess Chalil was not happy with the excuse he gave.

"Then you will have to accept all the results of your actions today." Chalil was shaking her head. "Good day, Prince Stellar. Your time to speak with me is now over."

The young prince bowed deeply, as was the way to say goodbye in Urania. Princess Chalil went down to start dancing with the princes whom she favored.

Prince Stellar slipped away to go to the chambers prepared for him. "Do you wish for us to draw you a bath?" The maidservant asked the prince.

"Oh, there is no need for that. I can take a bath in the outdoor baths, can I not?" He did not want to ask servants to carry so many pails of water to his room.

"But nobles are not supposed to use those baths. They are for the servants and peasants!" The maidservant has never heard of a noble doing that.

"In my home, I bathe in the waterfalls near our small castle. It is my preference to bathe outdoors. I do not wish for you to have to carry so many pails of hot water for me. Cold or hot, water is water. I just need to take all this mud off me." The smile he gave the maidservant made her heart swell. None of the young princes today ever gave more than two words to the servants.

"It is too bad..." the maidservant whispered.

"What is too bad?" Stellar asked the maidservant.

"It is too bad your first impression was not good. I think the queen and the princess don't like you because you came late and in such a state." The maidservant had to say it in a whisper since she was worried the castle spies would hear her.

Chapter 13: The Fairest of Them All

"I trust that the queen and princess are nicer than that. I have heard of how beautiful they all are, inside and out." He patted his chest then said, "Don't worry miss, I clean up quite well. So please tell me where the baths are located."

"If you bring your clothes, I shall show you where the men's bath is."

Stellar thought about the princess while he bathed. "Would she really not like me because I am not as polished as the men who came before me?"

When he finished his bath, he came back to the ballroom and saw that the princess was getting tired from all the dancing she had to do. He wanted to dance with her too. But it would have been too hard for her. He approached the orchestra and asked the musicians if they could play a song for him.

The song that was playing ended and the song he wanted started playing. He stood in front of the orchestra and put the spell on his throat that made it easy for everyone to hear him. He learned that spell for performing in his home. Spectacle Island was a small kingdom but the people loved music there.

Even if the princess didn't think he was a nice and polished royal, he wanted to gift her with a song on her birthday before he was eliminated from the princely race.

Everyone stopped when the prince began to sing. "If you are going to miss me as I pass you by, I wish for you to listen to this one lullaby." Princess Chalil gasped when she heard a wonderful and dreamy voice echoing in the ballroom.

"I have counted the days until I could meet you. This day was such a dream, seeing you was my hope. Even if from afar, your beauty blinds me. Even if I cannot be by your side, it doesn't stop me. I'll love you from a distance. You are an angel floating as you dance. Please teach me how to forget you. For all my days will be filled with thoughts of you."

The women in the hall all sighed when the song began to wane. The thunderous clapping followed a split second of silence once it finally ended. The orchestra was smiling and Prince Stellar bowed to the crowd.

He walked towards Princess Chalil, who was now in the middle of the ballroom. "I wish for you the happiest birthday, Princess Chalil. May you have many returns." He bowed in front of her and opened his palm to show her his gift.

"It's beautiful."

"The ring was made from elder wood. The ring will never ever fade. The Elder tree is my island's treasure."

"I can't have it then. It's so precious."

Chapter 13: The Fairest of Them All

"My mother told me when she gave it to me to only give it to the fairest of them all." Prince Stellar put the ring on Princess Chalil's right ring finger. "No matter whom you choose, I want you to have it. You are the fairest of them all…for me."

Princess Chalil looked at the ring, then back to Prince Stellar's face. "I loved your song."

"Did you? I changed the words to a song my father taught me. I wanted you to know what was in my heart. I am not good at talking. Singing is easier for me."

"It was amazing."

"I shall give you another song someday, with the melody and words made just for you."

"Is that a promise?"

"If you would like to hear it then yes, it's a promise."

"I shall want to hear your songs every day of my life then. That is my wish. Can you make that promise then?" Princess Chalil's words made the other princes feel defeated.

Stellar looked into Chalil's eyes, hoping to see if she meant every word of what she said. "You have only just met me, Princess. Do you not need to wait until you can get to know me better?"

"Our kingdom's king and queen fell in love in a day. We follow our elders well in Urania, don't you know?" Princess Chalil winked at Prince Stellar.

"What a fine tradition that is."

"Falling in love doesn't always take time, my prince. You had me at the first verse." Chalil laughed as Stellar held out his hand.

Their dance marked the end of the birthday party. Although the other princes were sad over the fact that another Uranian princess was taken, they could not fault the princess for falling in love with the golden voice of Stellar of Spectacle Island.

Chapter 14: Falling From Grace

A princess must always be graceful and sweet. Grace was anything but. She liked to play outside and run around in the forest. Her maids and guards were constantly trying to stop her from getting hurt.

"Princess, you mustn't be unruly. You have to be proper and feminine. No princess runs around in the woods and comes home all covered in twigs and mud." Rahja, her maidservant, was upset over her unladylike behavior.

"Must I always be proper? Must I be feminine to be a princess?" Grace asked Rahja. "I heard my mom was a bit like me growing up too. She grew up to be a great queen."

"That's because she learned a very hard lesson when she was young. She almost brought a curse down the whole kingdom because she didn't listen to her elders well."

"We can't have that. I wouldn't want a curse to come to Urania just because of me." Princess Grace loved her kingdom. Her father and mother always worked hard to keep Uranians happy.

"Well then, let's get you into a nice dress before you meet with your sisters and parents. The ministers will be there too. You must be a proper princess around them."

"Right. Then princess me up, Rahja. Make sure they don't mistake me for a misfit." Princess Grace grinned at her maidservant. It was fun to make the old lady panic.

Princess Grace always liked things outside of the definition of princess activities. She learned how to use magic from her father and the magi. She also learned how to protect herself from a bigger person. She made her guard teach her just in case someone tried to take her away against her will. Bandits were not uncommon in the lands around Urania. It was better to know than not know how to defend oneself.

"What you must do is find a hobby that is princess-like."

"Like what? Flower arrangement? Dressmaking? Painting?" She listed down the three things she was horrible in. "I would rather learn knots from the sailors then how to make designs on silk."

Rahja sighed, as if giving up any will to fight with the young princess.

Grace met with the ministers and the royal family in the throne room. There was a group of men who were kneeling in front of the king. "Untie them. They will not harm us here."

Chapter 14: Falling From Grace

"They are bandits who robbed the merchants on their way out of Urania. They are too dangerous to be kept unbound," the head of the king's guard said to the king.

"Untie them now! Bandits or not, they are Uranians too." The king's heart couldn't bear to see even a single one of his people bound and gagged.

One of the bandits got to his feet after getting untied. He grabbed Princess Grace, who was momentarily petrified from shock. "If you don't release my brothers then I will cut her throat!"

All the guards pointed their spears at the kneeling men. King Arell looked at Grace and winked. The princess held the poker knife, a thin pointed knife, and put pressure on the man's wrist. The bandit released the knife and the captor and hostage's roles were switched. "On your knees, bandit."

Even the ministers couldn't help but clap at the agility Princess Grace displayed. "Any last words, bandit?"

"Please do not forgive me. But please let my brothers go," he begged her. "I am without a child and a wife. But they have families to feed. We have been moving from town to town looking for work. But we could not find a place to stay. So we are staying in the mountains, waiting for merchants to pass by and trade with. The merchants we robbed were those who stole from the people. They bought all the goods at a small price and then when they owned all of the stocks, they would sell them for a higher price. I know what we did to them was wrong, but we were only trying to help the people too!"

"Doing another bad thing to undo a bad thing is never the solution." King Arell pulled his daughter into a comforting embrace. He took the pointed knife and threw it in front of the kneeling men. "What punishment do you think fits your crime?"

The bandit spoke up and said, "Anything short of taking our lives is right, Your Majesty."

"Then it is your life that I must take." The men started to wail. They did not want to die. They were all their families had. "You must take to the land and raise me cows and oxen. Make the land grow golden corn and rice. And in the months when there is no harvesting and planting, you must go to the mountains to find mushrooms, fruits, and truffles. Sell those to me and I shall give you a fair price."

The men all started rejoicing after hearing what the king said. The bandit asked, "But what land will we farm?" They were nomads who didn't have their own property.

"I am sure the merchants who stole from my people have land I can part them with. They won't be needing farmlands when they are spending time in the dungeon." King Arell became very serious. "A man who steals to eat for he is starved is merely trying to survive. A man who steals even

Chapter 14: Falling From Grace

when his coffers are full is the vilest creature in all of Urania. It is my life's goal to rid Urania of people like that."

The bandits were taken back to gather their family and start their life's work. The king faced Princess Grace with a worried look. "I know you are strong. But don't ever give me that kind of fright again, Princess."

Princess Grace laughed at the king's worried face. "I am your daughter. I cannot promise that I won't be brave."

The king looked at the queen and sighed. "Not very far from the apple tree, is she?" The king often said that an apple tree cannot bear peaches to refer to the similarity of the princesses to his queen.

Princess Grace is not a graceful or demure princess. But she was always true to herself. Accepting ourselves can help us love ourselves and others more. One does not have to fit the mold to be a good person, princess or not.

Chapter 15: Tiah's Sweets

It was the sweetest time in Urania; the month of sweet fruits being harvested has come. Princess Tiah loved to eat sweet things made from the fruits that grow on the land.

"I shall ask each cook to make me a dessert that will be served in royal banquets!" It was rare for a new recipe to be added to the royal cookbook, for the royals had to show even rare quality in the food they ate.

Bekah wanted to be a royal chef all his life. He had been learning how to be a cook from the town cook and the mothers in his hometown. He talked to every farmer and learned about all the food in Urania from travelers passing his town. He traveled to the capital in order to become a famous chef and gain an invitation to be a part of the royal kitchen. But it has been years and still, no invitation came. No matter how many noblemen and women came to his restaurant, the royal family never came to eat.

He took this new challenge as his last to become a royal chef. He was determined to make the best dessert for the princess. There was an added bonus too. If he impressed the king, he might gain the princess' hand in marriage. She was

Chapter 15: Tiah's Sweets

still young but if she grew to like him because of his skills, then he could gain her heart.

"The way to a woman's heart is through pastries." This was his motto and he knew Princess Tiah would not be any different.

When the Royal Dessert Battle came, chefs and cooks from all over Urania came to participate. They were all asked to bring a pastry or a dessert they made from their homes. Bekah brought his volcano cake. It was a simple moist muffin that had chocolate oozing out of it when one cut into it. He knew Princess Tiah was a chocolate lover. He put a bit of red-orange color into the chocolate and made it look like lava was coming out of the muffin.

Princess Tiah tasted each of the two hundred desserts that came. She would make marks on a parchment showing the score she gave each dessert. She didn't hear any of the explanations and washed her mouth with water after each tasting.

When it was Bekah's turn, he tried to explain the dessert. "It's like a volcano which spits out lava." He pointed at the middle of the muffin. "Please poke it here."

The princess did what he said and she saw the chocolate lava oozing out. "It's interesting." She tasted a bit of it and wrote down the score.

He didn't see any reaction from her so Bekah was worried. When the princess finished the tasting she gave the parchment to a royal announcer. The man was to read the score of each person. The princess used the numbers one to ten in order to grade each dessert. "All those whose score is below five will be eliminated." That part of the announcement made people more anxious. As the royal announcer said the scores, those who got five were so relieved that they cried. Those who got higher scores were proud of the result. But those who got four or lower walked away with slumped shoulders.

When Bekah's score was announced he was expecting to get a ten but the score was "Bekah of Puff Town, five!"

He was devastated. He was a master chef. He owned a luxurious restaurant. How could he get only a five?

"This is unacceptable," he whispered to himself. "The princess must be giving scores out of whim. She doesn't know a thing about cooking! She must have never lifted a finger in the royal kitchen."

The person next to him shook his head. "I heard the princess has a perfect palate."

Bekah formed an x with his arms. "There is no such thing as a perfect palate. It's a story people who can't get the right seasoning use as an excuse."

Chapter 15: Tiah's Sweets

"It's true! The King has supernatural powers that he was able to pass down to his daughters. Each one shows a power different from the others." The baker next to him was someone who worked in the capital for a long time. "When she was a young girl, she came to my shop and told me all the ingredients I used in my bread. She even gave me advice on how to make them better. I followed her advice and now I am doing well. The other cooks in the capital also experienced it."

"How come she never came to my restaurant?" He was suddenly very insulted.

"The princess comes and goes as she pleases. A magus gave her a transformation charm. She can look like a commoner and go to the stores as a traveler. She gives them advice if they need any."

"Then she must have thought my food was very good. She never said anything about my food."

"Actually..." The baker seemed unsure whether he should tell Bekah what he knew or not.

"Come out with it, man." Bekah was curious now.

"She said that your food lacks love."

"Love is not an ingredient! How can she even say that?" He was definitely insulted now.

"That is why she said she couldn't tell you. It's not something you can change." The baker completed his story.

Bekah looked at the princess who was enjoying tea while the rest of the scores were being announced. "She sits on her silly throne judging other people's food. My food does not lack love!"

The next challenge was held the next day. All they were asked to do was to think of the dessert they always wanted to eat. Bekah had a simple dessert in mind. It would surely make the princess think that loveless food was not his domain.

After the first challenge there were only twenty chefs left. All of them were worried they would get eliminated in this challenge.

Princess Tiah went into the kitchen where they were going to have the battle and greeted them with a sweet smile. "Good morning, dear chefs. Welcome to my private kitchen."

They were astonished with the luxurious kitchen. They didn't know the princess had her own kitchen in the palace. "Do you cook for the royal family often, Your Highness?"

"My family loves different kinds of food and so I had to learn a lot of different cuisine. Today's theme is family." The other chefs seemed happy but Bekah was more worried this time. He was an orphan who only knew his mother for ten years.

Chapter 15: Tiah's Sweets

He had grown up without a father. He was raised by an aunt who ran a small eatery. What had helped him become such a good cook and baker was that he had to learn so much to keep the prices of their ingredients at the lowest. His aunt worked so hard that she passed away at a young age too. So when she was gone, Bekah went to the capital to try his luck there.

"You have to make a dessert that you want to give to your family. It must be a dessert that is of your own making—not something that is similar to anything already found in the royal cookbook. The winner of this challenge will become a royal chef. This dessert will be served to royals and envoys that come to our land. People from all around Urania and even beyond our world will know of your great dessert."

The chefs were very happy to hear about the prize. But Bekah wanted something else. He wanted Princess Tiah to acknowledge him too. He knew he was going to be the winner, after all. "If the honor would be so great, then should you not give a gift to the winner too?"

"What gift would it be that you would wish for me to give?" Princess Tiah smiled at him despite feeling a bit flustered by this question.

"Your hand in marriage, when you come of age of course." The chefs there were mostly single men.

"What about me? I already have a wife. What do I gain if I win?" The baker Bekah talked to last time spoke up. The other married men also jeered.

"Then the princess can choose to marry your son or anyone whom you recommend." Bekah looked at the princess with mischief in his eyes.

One of the guards spoke up. "You overstep your ground, baker."

"It's alright, Markus." Princess Tiah calmed down the guard. She looked at Bekah and asked, "Is it your wish to marry me or is it your wish to be royal?"

Bekah was surprised with the princess' directness. Princesses are supposed to be demure and conventional. He forgot for a second that Princess Tiah is Queen Jina's daughter. The mother was once known as the Plague Bringer. It wouldn't be surprising that her daughters would have strong backbones.

"You must choose me first in order to find out." The other men smiled at Bekah's arrogant answer.

"Don't worry, Bekah. I shall make sure you don't get that chance," one of the chefs spoke out.

"Challenge accepted," Bekah teased them.

Chapter 15: Tiah's Sweets

The second challenge was harder because the stakes grew. "You have one hour to make your dessert. After which I will taste it. If you fail, you must leave the palace at once."

Bekah thought, *I have to win this one. Love is an ingredient. Then taste all the love you can't have if you don't choose me.*

The minutes ticked away and the other chefs finished their desserts. All of them were astonished with the dessert that Bekah made. It was dried summer fruits candy. It was not something original but it was shaped in the fruits' miniature forms.

Each man was given a chance to present their dessert to the princess and they explained their work as best as they could. This time the princess ate the desert and then shared it with the guards. She told the chef whether the dessert passed or not.

By the time it was Bekah's turn, all but one of the previous participants were eliminated. Only the baker whom he talked to had passed. Bekah was the last participant to show off his dessert.

"I made dried miniature candy," Bekah started his explanation. "When I was younger my mother passed away. My aunt, who owned an eatery in our town, raised me. She taught me how to cook so that I could never go hungry. She never gave me any desserts because we were barely able to get by. Once I went to work on a fruit farm and the farmer paid us in fruits. I brought them home and I asked my aunt to make me a pie with them. She refused and proceeded on drying the fruits and cutting them up. She placed them in a glass jar and told me to take out only one candy each day. The dried fruits lasted me a whole three months. Each day, I ate one at the end of the day and all of my exhaustion went away. When I was traveling to the capital, I brought a batch that I made. It was the last time I got to eat dried fruits from my hometown. I think people who come to Urania can bring them home with them and remember the times they had in our kingdom."

The guards who were there looked at the fruit candies with wet eyes. They knew the feeling of having to be away from their hometowns and family. The old baker was crying too.

Princess Tiah tasted the dessert and smiled. "You finally found the answer. You brought love back to your food!"

"I never lost it, Princess. But for a lonely man like me, I can't cry every time I cook. So I kept that very special ingredient for special occasions. When a family comes to my restaurant to celebrate their child's birthday, I give them the volcano cake I gave you before. It's the wonder and fascination of the person eating the food that makes the meal even more delicious."

Chapter 15: Tiah's Sweets

"Unfortunately, they do not win against the dragon fruit tarts that the baker made. His was a tastier pastry." The princess was not one to be swayed by a story.

The guards all grumbled against the princess' choice. They all wanted to taste the candies again. If it was included in the royal cook book, they could eat it in the palace too. The gods only knew when they could taste Bekah's fruit candies again.

"But as your dessert is actually a candy the people would love, I would like you to make them for the people of Urania. I do not wish for your delicious creation to be something only royals can eat. I want all of the people to eat it too."

The old baker became a royal chef and created different desserts that were added to the royal cook book. Meanwhile, Bekah created a long line of candies and desserts and named his shop, Tiah's Sweets. All around Urania and even beyond their world, all kinds of creatures came to buy the fruit candies that Princess Tiah loved.

One day when the store was about to close, a young woman came to ask for a box. Bekah was so tired that he didn't want to sell her anything. But the woman took down her robe's hood and said, "If you don't have any here, would you mind making some in the palace?"

Princess Tiah was her mother's daughter and she wasn't the kind to wait for him any longer. "I can make you some now."

Bekah felt all his tiredness disappear when the princess smiled at him.

"Can you make them for me, forever?" Bekah smiled and nodded. He took the princess' hand and put a candy ring on her left finger.

"Would you be my baking partner and my wife?" Princess Tiah nodded and they shared the sweetest of kisses.

Chapter 16: Royal Double Trouble

In the land of Urania, there are ten beautiful princesses. Each one grew to be smart, beautiful, but very playful. Princess Mara, Chalil, Tiah, Grace, Andera, Pia, Nana, and Meadow later outgrew their playfulness. But the Royal Duo, Princess Uno and Dos, never saw the need to grow up as they grew older.

Queen Jina spent a lot of time going through the things the twin princesses did. They've wreaked havoc in the palace for eighteen years. But the worst of them all came that evening. The palace was awoken by the guards trying to put out the fire in Princess Tiah's kitchen. Luckily no one was there. But the baker princess was in tears. Her carefully prepared ingredients and secret recipe book were all burnt in the fire.

The king was alarmed since the princess' kitchen was in the princesses' palace. It was impossible to get inside if they were not invited. The kitchen was under renovation so it was off-limits to everyone. Paint and other things were stored in the same place so as to minimize the work for the decorators.

"There shouldn't be anything that could start a spark in the kitchen. We took out the metals and the fire starters." The guards who were assigned to the kitchen were very sure about that.

Uno elbowed Dos who whimpered in pain. "What? Stop that. Father will see." Dos was afraid King Arell would notice.

She was not wrong. The king asked Dos and Uno what they were talking about. "Is there something you wish to ask, my dearest?"

Dos said, "Nothing, Father!"

Uno said, "Sorry, Father!"

King Arell asked everyone but the royal family to leave. "Now, let's hear why Uno is sorry."

"I cooked noodles in the kitchen, Father. I am sorry." Uno was trembling and crying. Dos started to cry to.

"No, Father, it was me. I cooked the noodles in the kitchen. But I tipped the charcoal and it rolled to the other side of the room. I didn't know where it went. I cleaned up the cooking pot and the other things. I went to get Uno and the guards but then a loud bang that came from the kitchen."

"Why didn't you ask for help as soon as you came out?" Tiah was still upset but was a bit relieved that her sister didn't get hurt.

"I was too scared. I am sorry, big sister." Tiah hugged Dos to comfort her. Uno hugged Dos too.

Chapter 16: Royal Double Trouble

The queen looked at the king and sighed. "It must be so hard for you to have daughters who are just like me."

"You gave me ten versions of you. I must be a very lucky man indeed." King Arell liked to tease the queen.

"Uno, is there something you want to tell us?" The queen faced the twin whose nose must have been getting longer from lying.

"I am sorry that I lied earlier. I didn't want Dos to get in trouble." Uno was the older twin. "I am the older sister, after all."

"You are only two minutes older, big sister!" Dos teased Uno, who always liked to be called big sister.

"I know that you love her very much. But even my father and mother didn't let me get away with doing bad things. I always got punished when I did something wrong." Queen Jina remembered the story of her ring.

"I never started a curse, mother," Dos teased Queen Jina.

"Talking back to your elders is also a bad thing to do, Princess," Queen Jina said in a somber voice.

Dos hugged the queen and asked for forgiveness. "I won't eat noodles for a month as punishment." The princess knew the king would ask her for the punishment she thought was fitting for what she did.

"No noodles for a month is a bit much." King Arell began to think. "I think that helping in cleaning the kitchen would be a better punishment. For the both of you."

Uno and Dos looked at their father with begging eyes. "That doesn't work when you are already eighteen," he said.

"What are you talking about, Your Majesty? Those eyes always work on you. The twins learned it from me," the queen teased the king, whose resolve was already breaking.

King Arell tried to be stubborn. He cleared his throat, then said, "For causing damage to the castle and destroying the copies of Princess Tiah's secret recipes, I hereby order that the Princesses Uno and Dos be made to clean the mess they made. They will be asked to clean the kitchen and restore the contents of Princess Tiah's recipe book." The king faced Princess Tiah. "Is this an ample punishment for the crime, my dear?"

Princess Tiah smiled at the king and then bowed in gratitude. "I shall teach them proper manners in the kitchen, Your Majesty."

The two princesses looked at the charred kitchen and sighed together. "This is going to take a lot of work."

King Arell patted each twin's back and said, "It should give you ample time to reflect on all your actions. Remember this, not even your sisters would let you get away with bad

Chapter 16: Royal Double Trouble

things. The whole kingdom looks to you to be good examples to other children. You must start growing up soon."

Uno and Dos helped Tiah with fixing the princess' private kitchen. They also learned all sorts of noodle dishes. Now, no one burns even a single muffin in that kitchen.

Conclusion

I'd like to thank you for reading Urania's fantastic tales.

I hope this book was able to help you to learn wondrous ways to life a full and happy life.

Now it's your turn to create stories of your own, and share them with others.

Thanks for reading!

Thank you

Before you go, I just wanted to say thank you for purchasing my book.

You could have picked from dozens of other books on the same topic but you took a chance and chose this one.

So, a HUGE thanks to you for getting this book and for reading all the way to the end.

Now I wanted to ask you for a small favor. **Could you please consider posting a review on the platform? Reviews are one of the easiest ways to support the work of independent authors.**

This feedback will help me continue to write the type of books that will help you get the results you want. So if you enjoyed it, please let me know.

www.ingramcontent.com/pod-product-compliance
Lightning Source LLC
LaVergne TN
LVHW020054080526
838200LV00083B/182